For Oslu Phipps II
With Best Whiskers!

Cheers!

MIZNER MOUSE
THE PRIDE OF PALM BEACH

Written by
Peter W. Barnes *and*
Cheryl Shaw Barnes

Illustrated by
**Anthony
Penta Kramer**

Other titles from VSP Books

Nat, Nat, the Nantucket Cat, about beautiful Nantucket Island, Mass.

Nat, Nat, the Nantucket Cat Goes to the Beach, the further adventures of Nat.

Woodrow, the White House Mouse, about the presidency and the nation's most famous mansion.

Woodrow for President, about how Woodrow got to the White House.

House Mouse, Senate Mouse, about Congress and the legislative process.

Marshall, the Courthouse Mouse, about the Supreme Court and the judicial process.

A "Mice" Way to Learn About Government teachers' curriculum guide.

Capital Cooking with Woodrow and Friends, a cookbook for kids that mixes fun recipes with fun facts about American history and government.

A "Mice" Way to Learn about Voting, Campaigns and Elections teachers' curriculum guide.

Alexander, the Old Town Mouse, about historic Old Town, Alexandria, Va., across the Potomac River from Washington, D.C.

Martha's Vineyard, about wonderful Martha's Vineyard, Mass.

Cornelius Vandermouse, the Pride of Newport, about historic Newport, R.I., home to America's most magnificent mansion houses.

Order these books through your local bookstore by title,
or order **autographed copies** by calling **1-800-441-1949**,
or from our website at **www.VSPBooks.com**.

For a brochure and ordering information, write to:

VSP Books
P.O. Box 17011
Alexandria, VA 22302

ISBN 1-893622-12-6

10 9 8 7 6 5 4 3 2 1

Printed in the United States of America

We dedicate this book to our friends in Palm Beach,
especially Thomas L. Phillips and Cameron Randall Phillips and their son, Reagan.

We wish to thank and acknowledge the help and assistance of Polly Earl,
executive director of the Preservation Foundation of Palm Beach,
and her entire staff in the production of this book.

—P.W.B. and C.S.B.

For my mother, Barbara, who introduced me to the finer things
in life at an early age and continues to be my inspiration
to live a fulfilling life. With abundant love and gratitude
from your "child" to last through a lifetime…and then some.

With special thanks to James McDaniel, the greatest
"transfer artist" an illustrator could hope for…bar none!

—A.P.K.

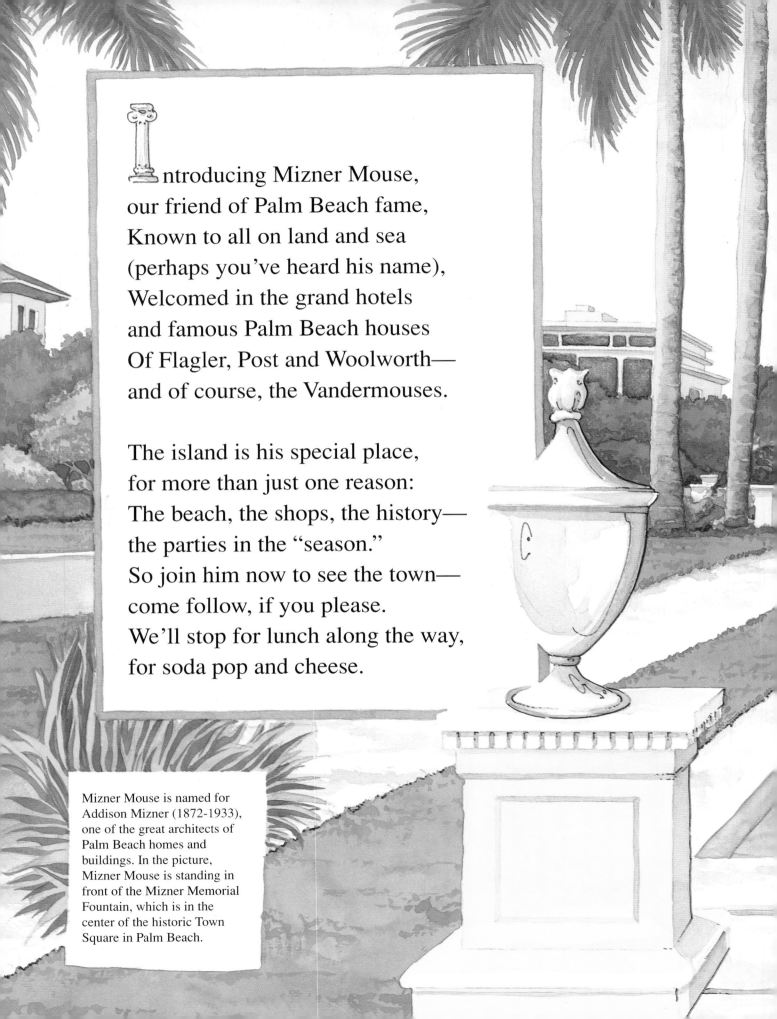

Introducing Mizner Mouse,
our friend of Palm Beach fame,
Known to all on land and sea
(perhaps you've heard his name),
Welcomed in the grand hotels
and famous Palm Beach houses
Of Flagler, Post and Woolworth—
and of course, the Vandermouses.

The island is his special place,
for more than just one reason:
The beach, the shops, the history—
the parties in the "season."
So join him now to see the town—
come follow, if you please.
We'll stop for lunch along the way,
for soda pop and cheese.

Mizner Mouse is named for
Addison Mizner (1872-1933),
one of the great architects of
Palm Beach homes and
buildings. In the picture,
Mizner Mouse is standing in
front of the Mizner Memorial
Fountain, which is in the
center of the historic Town
Square in Palm Beach.

We'll walk along Worth Avenue and do some window-shopping.
(Watch out, now, for once you start, there often is no stopping!)
The clothes! The jewels! The fancy shoes!
The marvelous antiques!
"Be careful with your credit cards,"
our tour guide, Mizner, squeaks.

Worth Avenue is the premier shopping street of Palm Beach. It is lined with many stores and shops. It was the site of Addison Mizner's first commission in Palm Beach, the Everglades Club, built in 1918.

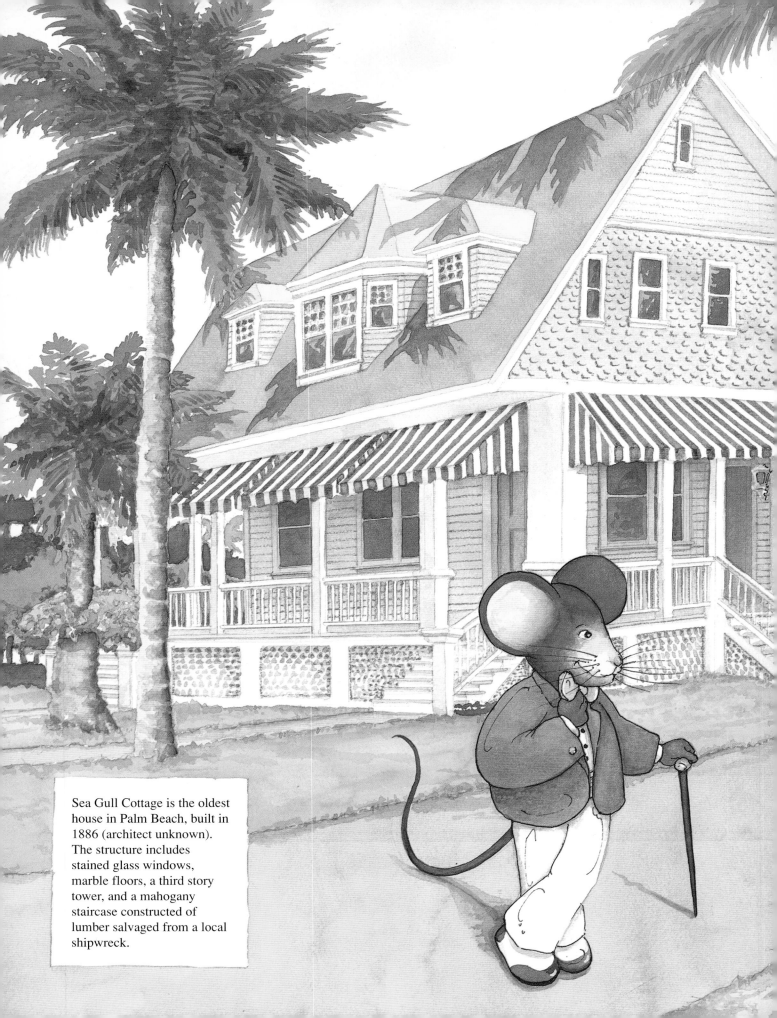

Sea Gull Cottage is the oldest house in Palm Beach, built in 1886 (architect unknown). The structure includes stained glass windows, marble floors, a third story tower, and a mahogany staircase constructed of lumber salvaged from a local shipwreck.

Mizner's home is not that far
—why don't we wander down?
Known as "Sea Gull Cottage,"
it's the oldest house in town!
It was built so long ago, in 1886,
When Palm Beach was a wilderness
of palm trees, shrubs and sticks.

Down the street a block or two
from where we first began,
We'll find a special garden
and a fellow known as Pan.
Made of bronze, he watches over
all the plants and flowers,
Day and night, in hot and cold,
in sun and gentle showers.

In his garden, look at all the
blossoms, fruits and trees,
Look at how the oak and cypress
rustle in the breeze.
There's a scarlet milkweed
and there goes a butterfly!
Three hundred different plants
and evergreens to please the eye.

Pan's Garden is a project of the Preservation Foundation of Palm Beach. Opened in 1994, it is a botanical garden devoted to Florida's native plants. It exhibits more than 300 different species of native plants in upland and wetland settings. More than 20 species of butterflies can be seen there.

The Little Red Schoolhouse, built in 1886, was the first schoolhouse in southeast Florida. It closed in 1901 but was restored in 1960. The Preservation Foundation of Palm Beach offers a special program at the Little Red Schoolhouse to all county schools.

A hundred years and more ago, the children of Palm Beach
All went to one place in town to hear their teachers teach:
The little schoolhouse, painted red, has only one large room,
Which made it rather crowded for the children, we presume!

Palm Beach offers visitors two public beaches, Phipps Ocean Park and Mid-Town Beach. Mid-Town Beach was the subject of an extensive beach restoration program, which helped create a habitat for sea turtles.

Walk along the sandy beach and see the palm trees swaying,
Everyone enjoys the day, see all the children playing.
Something splashes in the surf, then moves so quietly—
Why, it's a pretty sea turtle—it's swimming in the sea!

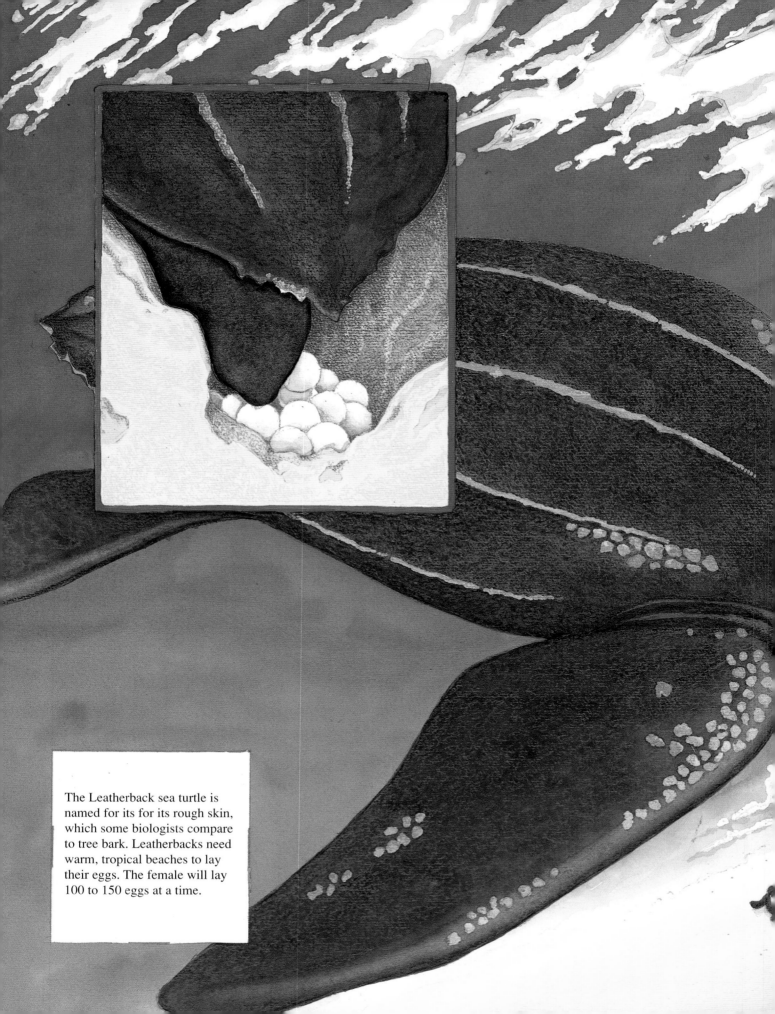

The Leatherback sea turtle is named for its for its rough skin, which some biologists compare to tree bark. Leatherbacks need warm, tropical beaches to lay their eggs. The female will lay 100 to 150 eggs at a time.

The turtles here are very rare
and must be treated well.
They call this one a "leatherback"
because it has a shell
That looks and feels like leather—
very hard and very thick.
A mother turtle swims ashore—
let's run to meet her, quick!

She clamors up the sand at night
to build herself a nest—
She digs a hole and lays her eggs—
she never takes a rest!
When she's done, she covers up the eggs
with lots of sand,
Then crawls back to the water
and swims off to other lands.

She lays a hundred eggs or more—
it really is a batch!
They lie six weeks inside the nest
and then the babies hatch!
They poke up through the sand and then—
a marvelous commotion,
To see them scamper off to start
their lives out in the ocean.

Down the beach there stands
"The Breakers"—what a grand hotel!
Visit and enjoy the food and service
nonpareil!

The waiters, maids and waitresses
are really very nice,
As are the clerks and managers,
the busboys and bellmice!

The Breakers is one of Palm
Beach's grandest and most
famous hotels. It has 560
rooms and sits on 140 acres;
the resort includes 36 holes
of golf and 10 tennis courts.
The hotel was built in the
Italian-Renaissance architectural style in 1926.

Mizner takes us to a very special house nearby—
The tower and chimneys climbing up to pierce the sky!
"Mar-A-Lago" it is called—it stands upon the earth
On a strip of land between the ocean and Lake Worth.

Mar-A-Lago, completed in 1927, is considered one of the most spectacular mansions in Palm Beach. It was built for socialite Marjorie Merriweather Post, the heiress of the Post cereal fortune. It was named a national historic landmark in 1972.

Known as "Whitehall," this old house is now a grand museum,
Filled with marbled rooms of gold (you really ought to see 'em!).

Whitehall, completed in 1901, is now home to the Flagler Museum, named for Henry Morrison Flagler, the oilman whose vision transformed Palm Beach into winter paradise. His private rail car, The Rambler, sits on the property.

The furniture and pottery, the art and chandeliers—
"You mustn't miss the ballroom, friends," Mizner volunteers.

Whitehall's gold ballroom was constructed and decorated in elaborate Louis XV style. It is one of 55 rooms in the house, which was a wedding gift from Henry Flagler to his third wife, Mary. It was built in just 18 months.

The Four Arts Library is the island's place for reading books,
Walk among the shelves and shelves and many reading nooks!
Read some new books, read your timeless favorites once again.
Mizner's favorite? Why of course, it is: *Of Mice and Men*.

The library, which opened in 1938, was designed by Maurice Fatio, a notable Palm Beach architect. The Society of the Four Arts was formed in 1934 to promote the arts and sciences.

Here's a special place that Mizner thinks is truly tops!
Look closely—you can see his name, right there above the shops!
"Via Mizner" honors not a mouse, but one great man
Who made the town one of the most enchanting in the land.

Villa Mizner, completed in
1924, was designed and built by
Addison Mizner for his private
office, residence, and studios.
The building was the first in the
complex of charming European
style shops known as Via
Mizner, which is just off Worth
Avenue. It helped turn Worth
Avenue into a special shopping
area.

Time for one last ride around in Mizner's silver Rolls,
One last chance to see the island's sites and cubbyholes.
He hopes you learned a thing or
two about Palm Beach, dear friend.
Please remember: DON'T be long
and DO come back again!

Today, Palm Beach remains one the world's most special and exciting places to shop, rest and play. But don't forget to also visit its special places and see its historic architecture, dominated by the work of Addison Mizner.

EDUCATIONAL NOTES FOR PARENTS AND TEACHERS

When Henry Morrison Flagler came to Palm Beach in the early 1890s, the island was a sparsely populated paradise of wild game, abundant fish and tropical plants. Flagler, a millionaire who had been a partner in Standard Oil, had come to Florida several years earlier with plans to make it a southern Newport, connecting resorts with his railroad, the Florida East Coast Railway. He opened his first Florida resort in St. Augustine in 1885.

In Palm Beach, Flagler especially liked the palm trees. In 1893, he decided to make it a stop on his railroad and laid plans for a new resort. He bought an existing house on the island, today known as Sea Gull Cottage (1886), which he lived in while he constructed his grand mansion, Whitehall (1901). In 1894, he opened his first Palm Beach property, the Royal Poinciana Hotel (demolished in 1934). His second hotel, the Palm Beach Inn, opened in 1895; he later enlarged it and renamed it The Breakers.

At time of Flagler's arrival, Palm Beach was populated mainly by hunters, fisherman and farmers. Residents founded their first school, the Little Red Schoolhouse, in 1886. Its first class consisted of seven students; the student body rose to 35 students in the 1890s. The schoolhouse was also home to the island's early religious services. The natives built their first church, Bethesda-By-The-Sea, in 1889.

As Flagler's plan blossomed, other visionaries stepped in to build Palm Beach into a premier winter resort. In 1918, Paris Singer, an heir to the Singer sewing machine fortune, joined forces with Addison Mizner, the brilliant architect. Mizner was born in California in 1872 and spent part of his childhood living in Guatemala, which gave him an appreciation of Spanish art and architecture. He formally trained as an architect in San Francisco, worked in New York City and traveled in Central America, the Orient, and Europe before settling in Palm Beach. In Palm Beach, he recognized that northern-style architecture was inappropriate for the island's lush, tropical environment. Instead, he introduced the romantic Spanish- and Mediterranean-influenced styles that dominate the island's architecture today, with many homes and structures that are recognized as historic landmarks. His first project for Singer was the famous Everglades Club (1918). The project led to commissions for several houses, and thus Addison Mizner's place in architectural history was assured. As wealthy families flocked to the island, other architects followed—John Volk, Howard Major, Maurice Fatio and Marion Sims Wyeth—but it was Addison Mizner who dominated the architectural scene in Palm Beach until his death in 1933.

Today, Palm Beach remains a popular destination for thousands of winter residents, vacationers and travelers each year, offering them beautiful accommodations, high quality restaurants and superlative shopping experiences. For more information, contact the Palm Beach Chamber of Commerce at 561-655-3282. Enjoy!

THE PRESERVATION FOUNDATION OF PALM BEACH

The Preservation Foundation of Palm Beach is a 501(c)3 charity and membership organization incorporated in 1979 to preserve the architectural heritage and the unique residential quality of the Town of Palm Beach. With over 1,200 local members, the Foundation offers a variety of programs for local school children, lectures and tours for adults, and supports local issues that preserve the character of the town. The Foundation also maintains Earl E. T. Smith Preservation Park, an urban green space; Pan's Garden, a botanical garden devoted to native Florida plants, and an archive and library of historical and architectural records. For membership or other information, please contact the Foundation at 561-832-0731.